THIS IS THOR

Adapted by Brooke Dworkin

Interior illustrated by Val Semeiks *and* Hi-Fi Design

Based on the Marvel comic book series Thor

New York
Los Angeles

All Rights Reserved. Published by Marvel Press, an imprint of Disney Book Group. No part of this book may be reproduced or transmitted in any form or by any means, electronic or mechanical, including photocopying, recording, or by any information storage and retrieval system, without written permission from the publisher.

For information address Marvel Press, 1101 Flower Street, Glendale, California 91201.

ISBN 978-1-4847-1268-9
G658-7729-4-14074
Printed in the United States of America.
First Edition
1 3 5 7 9 10 8 6 4 2

SUSTAINABLE FORESTRY INITIATIVE

Certified Chain of Custody
Promoting Sustainable Forestry

www.sfiprogram.org
SFI-01415
The SFI label applies to the text stock

This is Thor.

Thor is a prince.

His father is King Odin.

Thor has a brother.
His name is Loki.

Loki is a trickster.

Thor is Odin's favorite son.
Loki is jealous of Thor.

Thor and Loki live on Asgard.
It is a planet in space.

Asgard is connected to Earth.
They are linked
by the Rainbow Bridge.

Thor has three friends.
They are called
the Warriors Three.

Thor fights many
beasts and monsters.

He and Loki protect Asgard
from many enemies.

Thor has a
magic hammer.

The hammer was a
gift from Odin.

The hammer is heavy.
Thor could not lift it.

Thor had to earn the hammer.
He had to be brave.
He had to be honest.

Thor had to prove
that he was strong.

Finally Thor could
lift the hammer!

Thor throws his hammer.
It flies back to him.

Thor twirls his hammer
to fly through the sky.

Thor stamps his hammer
on the ground.
Lightning and thunder
fill the sky.

Thor is very proud
of his hammer.

He uses it to
protect Asgard.

Thor has a secret.
Sometimes he
lives on Earth.

Thor was sent to Earth
by his father.

Thor's name on Earth
is Don Blake.

He is a doctor.

Thor uses his powers
to protect Earth.

And he always will.